Bratz
Clued In!

Breaking
News

by Laura J. Burns

Grosset & Dunlap

GROSSET & DUNLAP
Published by the Penguin Group
Penguin Group (USA) Inc., 375 Hudson Street, New York, New York 10014, U.S.A.
Penguin Group (Canada), 90 Eglinton Avenue East, Suite 700, Toronto, Ontario,
Canada M4P 2Y3 (a division of Pearson Penguin Canada Inc.)
Penguin Books Ltd, 80 Strand, London WC2R 0RL, England
Penguin Ireland, 25 St Stephen's Green, Dublin 2, Ireland
(a division of Penguin Books Ltd)
Penguin Group (Australia), 250 Camberwell Road, Camberwell,
Victoria 3124, Australia (a division of Pearson Australia Group Pty Ltd)
Penguin Books India Pvt Ltd, 11 Community Centre, Panchsheel Park,
New Delhi – 110 017, India
Penguin Group (NZ), Cnr Airborne and Rosedale Roads, Albany,
Auckland 1310, New Zealand (a division of Pearson New Zealand Ltd)
Penguin Books (South Africa) (Pty) Ltd, 24 Sturdee Avenue,
Rosebank, Johannesburg 2196, South Africa

Penguin Books Ltd, Registered Offices:
80 Strand, London WC2R 0RL, England

 www.bratzpack.com

Used under license by Penguin Young Readers Group. Published in 2006 by Grosset &
Dunlap, a division of Penguin Young Readers Group, 345 Hudson Street, New York, New York
10014. GROSSET & DUNLAP is a trademark of Penguin Group (USA) Inc. Printed in the U.S.A

Library of Congress Cataloging-in-Publication Data

Burns, Laura J.
  Breaking news / by Laura J. Burns.
    p. cm. — (Clued in! ; #3)
  "Bratz."
  ISBN 0-448-43965-4
  I. Title. II. Series.
PZ7.B937367Bre 2006
[Fic]—dc22

                              2005021698

10 9 8 7 6 5 4 3 2 1

Breaking
News

Chapter 1

"I can't wait for journalism class tomorrow!" Cloe cried.

"Me either," her friend Jade replied from the next dressing room. It was Sunday afternoon, and Cloe, Jade, Yasmin, and Sasha were shopping at Funky Fashions. It was one of their favorite stores at the mall because it always had all the hottest clothes.

All four girls were taking a TV journalism class at their school, Stiles High. One of the coolest things about Stiles High was that there were television monitors in every classroom. Each day, the morning announcements were aired over these monitors. And this semester, everyone in the TV journalism class would be divided into teams and each would have the chance to produce its own segment following the announcements for a week.

"I'm so glad that it's finally our team's turn to get in front of the camera!" Yasmin added.

"I'm just digging the excuse to buy new clothes," Sasha said. She was checking out a shrunken blazer in the three-way mirror. "I could get used to this professional look."

Jade strutted out of the dressing room doing her best runway-model walk. She flipped her long black hair over her shoulder and grinned at Sasha and Yasmin. They made room at the mirror for her.

"Do you guys think we'll win the contest?" Yasmin asked.

"With all of us working together, how could we not?" Jade exclaimed.

Whichever team snagged the highest ratings from their fellow students would win a weekly segment on the *real* local morning news.

"Can you imagine us on *Rise and Shine?*" Cloe asked. She came out of her dressing room and did a little twirl so her friends could check out her ruffled mini. "Everyone in town will see us!"

"Our format is so fresh and different—it's got to earn us good ratings," Yasmin said.

The girls were planning to do their stories as a group, with all of them on-camera at once.

The other teams in their class had copied the format of a regular news show, with only one anchorperson delivering the report.

"We're so comfortable with one another that we'll have a blast doing our reports," Cloe said. "And the viewers will have fun watching us because we'll be having so much fun!"

"I wonder why Tamara didn't want to come shopping with us," Jade said. "It would have helped us get to know her better." Tamara was another member of their journalism team, along with two of their best guy friends, Cameron and Eitan. The four girls and two guys had chosen to work together, but Tamara had just been assigned to their team. She was new at Stiles High, so she didn't have anyone else to partner up with.

"Maybe she already has an outfit for tomorrow," Sasha replied.

"It would have been nice to bond a little, though," Cloe said. "If we're not comfortable together, there's no way our format will work."

"Well, we invited her to come," Jade pointed out. "But she's really kept to herself ever since she joined the team."

"Maybe she's just shy," Yasmin said.

"She never really liked the idea of our format, remember?" Sasha asked. "She seemed nervous about us all being on the air at once. Maybe she's mad that we're not doing the show the way everyone else did."

"But we voted," Jade said. "And the majority

of us like the format. Even the guys thought it would totally rock."

"She seemed okay with our final decision," Jade added. "She was probably just busy this afternoon."

"Probably." Cloe added a maroon leather cap to her outfit and smiled at herself in the mirror. The dark color looked great against her blond hair. "Too bad we can't have Cameron on-camera with us," she added.

Her friends exchanged knowing looks. It was so obvious that Cameron and Cloe liked each other, but they never admitted it.

"What?" Cloe demanded.

"Nothing, Angel!" Jade said. "But we do have to have a news producer, and Cameron is perfect for the job. He's so organized."

"And he's always so calm," Sasha said. "He'll be perfect behind the scenes, making sure our broadcast goes smoothly."

"But Cameron looks great on film," Cloe said with a sigh. "And he would give us the guy's point of view."

"Don't worry. Eitan's got it covered with his 'Guy Stiles' segment," Jade reminded her.

"I can't wait for that part!" Sasha was so excited that she busted a move. "He'll give all the guys tips on how to be stylin', just like he is!"

"*You're* stylin' in that jacket," Yasmin cried. "It will look great with your new white jeans."

"Thanks, Yas," Sasha said. "And that top is gorgeous on you."

"The neckline is so cool and different," Cloe agreed, checking out the asymmetrical collar on Yasmin's T-shirt.

"What about Jade's scorchin' leopard-print skirt?" Yasmin said. Everybody oohed and aahed at Jade's sizzlin' look—she always put together the hottest outfits!

"I'm definitely buying it for our big debut," Jade said.

"Perfect! So, the script's all written for tomorrow's report," Cloe said. "And now we all have amazin' outfits. Is that everything? Do you guys think we're ready?"

"Totally!" her three best friends cried.

Cloe grinned. "It's going to be the best show in the history of Stiles High!"

Chapter 2

Cameron and Eitan were waiting inside the television studio the next morning. "Showtime, everyone!" Eitan announced when he saw the girls. "Ready?"

"*So* ready," Jade told him. Yasmin nodded, bouncing up and down on her wedge-heeled sandals.

"How about you, Cameron?" Cloe asked.

"Whatever," Cameron mumbled. His head was buried in his notebook. "I have to study for my music theory test."

"Cameron's applying for an internship

at Sunburst Records," Eitan explained. "It's supercompetitive. Everybody wants to work at a real recording company!"

"I have to get an A in my music theory class, or they won't even consider me for the spot," Cameron said. "And I have a test on Friday."

"I'm sure you'll do great," Cloe said, but Cameron didn't even look up. Cloe couldn't believe it. Cameron had never ignored her like that before.

"Hi," a quiet voice said. The girls turned to see Tamara standing behind them. She was wearing a blue T-shirt and cropped jeans with frayed edges.

"Hey, girl!" Jade greeted her. "I love your jeans."

"Thanks," Tamara said. Then she turned and walked away.

Jade frowned. *What is Tamara's problem?* she wondered. Cloe took her arm and whispered, "I'm sure she's just nervous." Then in a louder voice she added, "Tamara's headed for makeup— and we need to get over there, too."

Every week, while one team did the show, the rest of the class worked behind the scenes, running the cameras, sound equipment, and teleprompter. They did everything that a real TV-news-show crew would do, including makeup for anyone going on-camera. This week, a girl named Kath was in charge of that.

"Ready for makeup?" Kath asked Tamara.

"I just want lip gloss," Tamara said.

"We'll need more than that to go onscreen," Cloe said. "The bright lights will make us all look pale."

"*All* of you need makeup?" Kath cried. "Why?"

"It's our show's format," Jade told her. "We're all hosting together."

"That's weird." Kath frowned and handed Tamara a tube of cherry-red lip gloss. "My team didn't do that. We just had one anchorperson."

Cloe sat in the makeup chair, and Kath started applying some sparkly orange eye shadow. "Can you use blue instead?" Cloe asked. "To match my eyes?"

Kath frowned, but she switched to blue. "We didn't need to do anything weird like you guys," she said. "We got great ratings anyway. My team will totally win the spot on *Rise and Shine*."

Jade rolled her eyes as she waited for her turn. Kath was really competitive. Everybody else in the class was totally cool and supportive of other teams, but Kath bragged about her team whenever she had the chance.

Sasha came over just as Tamara finished putting on her lip gloss.

"Want me to finish your makeup, Tamara?" Sasha asked. "I have green mascara. It will really make your eyes pop. They're such a great hazel color."

Tamara backed away. "I don't wear mascara."

Sasha didn't know what to say.

"I think it'd look really good, too," Cloe put

in. "And you can take it off as soon as the show's over."

Tamara shrugged. "I guess that'd be okay."

"I'll do it," Kath said. "It's my job." She grabbed the mascara out of Sasha's hand and began applying it. But she did it so quickly that she jabbed Tamara in the eye with the wand.

"Ow!" Tamara yelped.

"Sorry," Kath said. "I hope that doesn't make your eye all red. That would look pretty bad on-camera."

Jade didn't think Kath sounded sorry at all. She was being really mean! "I have a kickin' beaded necklace that will look amazin' with your T-shirt," Jade told Tamara, trying to cheer her up. "Do you want to borrow it?"

"No." Tamara rubbed her eye. She seemed more annoyed with Jade than with Kath.

Jade looked at Cloe. Cloe shrugged. Tamara just didn't seem to want to be friends with them.

As soon as their makeup was finished, it was time for the show to start.

Jade, Cloe, Sasha, Yasmin, and Tamara sat in five chairs on the stage, and Eitan was waiting backstage for his cue. Each of them wore a tiny earphone so they could hear Cameron giving them instructions through his radio. He would be in the control room watching the broadcast. Since he was the producer, it was his job to fix any mistakes that happened during the show.

Once they were settled in on the stage, the girls waited for Cameron to greet them over their headphones, but he wasn't in the booth. *Where could he be?* they wondered. At the very last second, Cameron rushed into the control room and spoke into the mike. "Ready?" he asked through their headsets. He sounded distracted.

All the girls nodded, relieved that he'd made it.

"Here we go," Cameron said. "Three, two, one . . ."

Cameron pushed a button on the computer and a title card appeared onscreen. Cloe had been chosen to design it on her computer because she was such a good artist. The card had funky lettering that read, "The Fashionable Five with Today's Topic: Dirty Laundry."

One of their classmates pointed the camera

at them, and then the girls were on the air!

Cloe read their script from the teleprompter. "What's up, Stiles High? It's Cloe, Sasha, Tamara, Yasmin, and Jade comin' at ya with today's hot scoop."

"We're talking about uniforms," Tamara said quietly.

"Speak up a little," Cameron said through their earphones.

"Gym uniforms," Tamara said in a louder voice, blushing.

"You know them—the ugly T-shirts and baggy shorts we all have to wear," Sasha said.

"You mean the *scratchy* T-shirts and shorts," Jade added. That line wasn't on the teleprompter because it wasn't in the script. But the girls had memorized most of their lines, so they felt comfortable improvising.

"That's right, Jade," Yasmin said. "Lots of people have been complaining about the uniforms lately. They've never been so stiff and uncomfortable before."

"And we found out why!" Cloe said.

"It took a lot of snooping and an extreme knowledge of fabric," Tamara read from the teleprompter. "But we did it."

"The uniforms are pure cotton, which means they should be comfy," Sasha said.

"But when washed in a harsh detergent, cotton gets stiff," Jade said.

"And you heard it here first," Yasmin went on. "The gym laundry switched to a cheaper detergent this year—"

"Cheap is good. But this detergent isn't," Cloe ad-libbed.

Tamara hesitated. She had the next line, but she seemed confused by Cloe's interruption. "Um, the new soap makes the uniforms scratchy and uncomfortable," Tamara read.

"And not just the gym suits. It's the sports team uniforms, too," Jade added. "So come on, Stiles High. Help us protest the new laundry detergent, and protect your fellow students from game-time scratchiness. We're putting a petition in the front lobby, along with a list of other detergents that are just as cheap but work way better."

"When we have enough signatures, we'll

send it to the school board," Tamara read.

"Drop by and give us your autograph," Sasha said. "Help us make PE more comfortable for everyone!"

Yasmin looked straight into the camera. She didn't need to read the script at all for the next part. "You've heard the news. Now let's talk about the uniforms! Why do we have mandatory gym suits at all? Is it a good rule or a bad one?"

"In my opinion, it's a bad rule," Jade replied. "Everybody has their own sense of style, even at the gym! The uniforms don't let people express themselves. Plus, they went out of fashion five years ago."

All the girls laughed, even Tamara. That last part wasn't in the script either, but Jade and

Yasmin were such good friends that it was easy for them to throw in a few spontaneous comments. It was just like they were having a regular fashion chat!

"It's true that the uniforms aren't the most fashionable," Yasmin said. "But maybe that's good. Some people haven't found their personal style yet—"

"Or they're insecure," Tamara interrupted.

Yasmin was surprised. Tamara hadn't said a single unscripted thing yet. But she had a great point. "Right!" Yasmin cried. "The required uniforms are good because nobody has to worry about looking unfashionable or feeling insecure about their workout clothes. Everyone looks the same."

"I can see both sides of the argument," Sasha

said. "But we can all agree on one thing."

"What's that?" Cloe asked.

"That the gym suit needs a major redesign," Sasha answered.

"That's why we're unveiling our designs for an all-new, way-cool gym uniform right here on the Stiles High morning show!" Jade announced.

With a flourish, Yasmin, Cloe, and Sasha each pulled drapes off of easels displayed on the stage, revealing their design sketches for several sleeker, hipper new uniforms. The five girls had worked together on all of the designs, and they were hoping the school board would go for one of them.

"Go to the Stiles High website to vote for your fave outfit!"

"Now let's hear the guy's point of view," Tamara read from the teleprompter. "Here's Eitan with some suggestions for the boys."

Eitan came out wearing the gym uniform, then demonstrated some ways to make it cooler by layering the T-shirt with other kinds of shirts. The girls thought the different variations were great.

All the girls had a great time chiming in on Eitan's piece. Before they knew it, Cameron called "Cut!" into their earphones.

Their first morning report was over. The girls and Eitan high-fived one another in excitement. The show had been totally amazing!

Chapter 3

At lunchtime, Sasha went to the school library to interview Mr. McNicholls, the advisor for their upcoming class trip to France. Sasha took notes in her zebra-print notebook. The girls were going to announce the trip on their next show.

"Make sure to tell everyone that this is a special trip," Mr. McNicholls said. "We usually go to Washington, D.C. But your class raised so much money that we can afford to go to Europe this year!"

"That's so awesome," Sasha said, diligently

writing down the teacher's quote. As Mr. McNicholls described all the places their tour would take them, Sasha got more and more excited. This would be the coolest TV report ever—all the kids in her class were going to be so psyched. It was the trip of a lifetime!

Meanwhile, Yasmin and Jade followed their friend Dylan around the cafeteria. He was taking the daily student survey about that morning's show.

Dylan went up to each table in the cafeteria and asked everybody to rate the morning's show on a scale of one to ten. Their show got almost all tens—and absolutely everybody wanted to see more of them in the future!

Yasmin and Jade squeezed each other's

hands in quiet celebration. "If the survey is any indication, we'll definitely win the contest and get a spot on *Rise and Shine*. It's our dream come true!" Jade cried.

Cloe pushed open the door of the student government office. Tamara followed her inside. They were there to meet the class treasurer, Cloe's friend Koby.

"Hey, Angel," Koby greeted her.

"Hi, Koby. Do you know Tamara?" Cloe asked.

"Only from your amazin' show this morning." Koby smiled at Tamara. "You guys were the best!"

Tamara just nodded and glanced nervously around the room.

"Thanks!" Cloe told Koby, trying to cover for Tamara's unfriendliness. "Tomorrow's show will be even better. We get to announce to the school that we're going to France this year."

"How cool is that?" Koby said. "Don't you think it's awesome, Tamara?"

"I guess," Tamara said.

Koby gave Cloe a questioning look. Cloe shrugged. She wanted to give Tamara the benefit of the doubt, but sometimes it seemed like the girl was just plain rude.

"So what do you guys need from me?" Koby asked.

"The basic 411 on how our class raised

enough money for the France trip," Cloe said. "I know the fashion show Jade organized last month helped!"

"It sure did, Angel," Koby agreed. "All the clothes sold for a lot of money."

Cloe wrote that down in her sketchbook. The book was officially for artwork, but Cloe used it for everything—notes to her friends, her to-do list, lots of doodles, and ideas for paintings. And now info for the team's reports!

"The tickets to the last party Dylan and Cade threw at Trax raised almost as much," Koby added. "Did you go to that party, Tamara?"

Tamara jumped as if she hadn't been paying attention. "Um . . . no," she muttered.

"How about the art fair?" Cloe asked. "Every single student painting and sculpture was sold."

"That event raised the most money of all," Koby said. "Even I bought a painting for my room!"

He listed all the clubs and special events that had raised money, and Cloe wrote them all down. She wanted to make sure everyone got credit for doing their part. But when she looked at Tamara, she wasn't even taking notes.

Tamara wasn't being any help at all!

Chapter 4

"Congratulations, everyone," Mr. Mazzei, the journalism teacher, said on Tuesday morning. "Your team's show yesterday got the highest ratings of any report so far."

"Awesome!" Eitan cried. He slapped Cameron on the arm triumphantly, but Cameron didn't respond. He was busy doing his music theory homework.

Cloe grinned at her friends, and they all smiled back—except Tamara. She looked as serious as usual, like she wasn't even happy about the news.

"Is everybody ready for today's show?" Sasha asked as they headed over to makeup.

"Totally," Cloe replied. "If today's show is as good as yesterday's, we'll definitely win the contest!"

"Don't count on it," Kath said as Cloe sat down. "I can't believe you guys got such high ratings—I think it's just 'cause people like you. I bet they weren't even watching."

Cloe gasped. "What do you mean?"

"The show was so confusing with all of you talking at once." Kath brushed some wine-colored blush onto Cloe's cheeks. "Today, everyone will realize that your format is weird. There's no way you'll win. It's not a popularity contest, you know."

"We never thought it was," Yasmin said, confused.

Cloe frowned at her reflection in the mirror. The blush was way too dark for her. Why did Kath keep using such bad makeup on them?

"Can you use a lighter color?" she asked.

"Whatever." Kath rolled her eyes and switched to another blush. "I'm so relieved you didn't pick me for your team."

"What are you talking about?" Sasha asked.

"You chose Tamara and not me," Kath said. "So I got to be on a normal team instead of being with you and your weird format."

Yasmin and Sasha shared a look. Tamara had been assigned to their team, but apparently

Kath didn't know that. They waited for Tamara to defend them and their format, but she didn't.

Cloe didn't know what to say. Tamara obviously wasn't happy she'd been put on their team. And Kath seemed to be the only one in the whole school who hadn't liked their gym-suit report.

There was an awkward silence while Kath did makeup for each of them. Even Eitan got a little powder so he'd look his best on-camera. But when it was Tamara's turn, she refused all but the bare minimum again.

Cameron stalked over from the control booth. "Where's Jade?" he demanded.

Jade rushed in with the script. "I'm finished fact-checking!" she said. "I had to swing by Koby's locker to check on one fund-raising number. It didn't make sense to me, and it turned out we put an extra zero on there!"

"You mean I have to change the script?" Cameron complained. "What a pain."

"Well, I had to run around like crazy to finish the fact-checking," Jade pointed out. "That was a pain, too."

"You don't get it," Cameron said. "None of you have any idea how much work it is to be the producer! And I don't even get to be on-camera and have fun like the rest of you."

Cloe shot him a disappointed look. What was wrong with Cameron lately? He was being totally unfair! "We've *all* done a ton of work," she said.

"Fine. I'll change it." Cameron grabbed the corrected script and rushed off.

The girls looked at one another and shrugged. Everybody seemed to be in a bad mood today.

Soon it was showtime. Cameron ran the new title card Cloe had designed. It said, "The Fashionable Five with Today's Topic: *Bonjour*, Stiles!"

"*Bonjour*, Stiles," Tamara read from the teleprompter. "Just to mix things up, today we're going to start out with our 'Guy Stiles' segment. Here's Eitan."

Eitan bounded out onto the set and did a rockin' segment on one of the hottest styles at school. Boys had started wearing bandannas tied around their arms. Eitan demonstrated a few different ways to tie them.

"That's cool," Jade cried, jumping up from her seat. "Tie one on my arm. There's no reason girls can't get in on a kickin' fad like this!"

Eitan wrapped a red bandanna over the sleeve of Jade's manga T-shirt. It looked perfect!

Then it was time for the big France announcement. The opening lines were Tamara's, but she was so busy watching Jade and Eitan that she didn't realize it was her cue. Jade knew that her messing around with Eitan had probably thrown her teammate off. "Now here's Tamara with a huge announcement," she ad-libbed.

Tamara blushed. She turned toward the teleprompter and began to read. "Hey, Stylin'

Stilers," she said. "It's time for the news you've all been waiting for—our class trip."

"This year, our class raised enough money to go someplace incredibly exciting," Cloe said.

"France!" they all cried together.

"Just imagine: Paris, the capital of fashion, art, and cooking," Yasmin said.

"Picture our class sampling the famous shopping on the Champs-Élysées," Sasha added.

"Or checking out amazin' works of art at the Musée d'Orsay," Cloe added.

"Plus hitting the castle at Versailles, a totally important historical site," Jade said.

"Unfortunately, we can't do any of it," Tamara said. "Because the funding is gone."

"What?" Cloe cried.

Tamara jumped in surprise, looking at Cloe.

"What are you talking about?" Cloe whispered.

Tamara squinted at the teleprompter. "Um … the funding is gone," she repeated. "Somebody stole the money from the school safe. The trip to France is canceled."

Jade frowned. "But that's not true," she said.

"Jade …" Yasmin nodded toward the camera. They were still on the air.

"The money is fine," Jade insisted.

"What's going on? What are you guys doing?" Cameron asked through their headsets.

Cloe looked at the teleprompter. It had already scrolled to the next page, and the words it showed were the words of the correct script. So why had Tamara said the trip was canceled? Was she trying to ruin their report?

"We'll have two whole weeks in France. It'll be the rockingest class trip in the history of Stiles High," Jade said brightly, trying to cover their confusion.

"But Tamara just said the trip was canceled," Cameron said through the headsets. All of their journalism classmates were staring at them in disbelief.

"It's not really canceled," Yasmin answered. She forgot that no one in the audience could hear Cameron. "I don't know why Tamara said that."

Tamara's cheeks burned beet-red. "Because it was in the script that *you* wrote," she cried.

"Chill, girls," Cloe murmured. "We're still on."

Yasmin clapped her hand over her mouth. She was so upset that she'd totally forgotten there was a camera on them.

Sasha looked at the camera. Their script was still up on the teleprompter, but continuing to talk about France didn't seem like a good idea. It might confuse their viewers even more.

"We're out of time," Cameron said into their headphones. "Cut!"

The red light on the camera went dark. They were off the air.

Nobody in the whole studio said a word. They didn't have to. The girls knew the truth: Their show had been a disaster!

Chapter 5

Sasha turned to Tamara. "Why did you do that?" she asked. "You ruined our show!"

Tamara just turned and ran out of the room. The other kids began shutting down the camera and sound equipment and turning off the bright stage lights. Cameron burst out of the control booth and hurried to join the rest of his team.

"What happened up there?" he asked.

"Yeah," Eitan said. "You guys seemed really disorganized."

"Tamara said something that wasn't true," Jade told them. "And once she said it, we couldn't figure out how to tell everyone it was a lie."

"We all got confused," Yasmin put in.

Cloe looked at the sad faces of her friends. "It's okay," she said. "We have three more days this week. Our reports will be amazing, and the ratings for today's show won't matter." She was trying to cheer them up, but even she couldn't help feeling awful.

"Cloe, Jade?" Mr. Mazzei called. "Can I see your whole team in my office?"

"Uh-oh," Sasha murmured. "That's not good."

"Do you think he's going to yell at us?" Cameron asked. "I can't be late for my next class—it's music theory. The teacher gives bad grades for lateness."

"Cam, we might be in trouble," Cloe pointed out.

He shrugged. "My music grade is more important than this."

Cloe frowned and led the way into Mr. Mazzei's office. "Where's Tamara?" he asked.

"She ran off," Yasmin replied.

"No, I'm right here." Tamara came in. Her eyes were red, and it looked like she'd washed all her mascara off.

"What happened during your report?" Mr. Mazzei asked.

"Tamara lied," Jade told him.

"I did not!" Tamara gasped.

Sasha frowned. "Then why did you say the France trip was canceled?"

"I just read the script from the teleprompter," Tamara said.

"None of that stuff was in the script," Yasmin said. "I know, I wrote it!"

"And I fact-checked it this morning," Jade put in.

"Whatever happened, it was not a professional report," Mr. Mazzei said. "The principal called asking why you girls were making up your facts. This is a very serious situation."

"We can do a retraction on tomorrow's show," Cloe suggested. "We'll recheck all our facts and tell everyone not to worry."

But Mr. Mazzei shook his head. "Today's report was embarrassing for the whole class. I'm going to put another team on the air tomorrow. I want you all to watch them closely and try to learn how to work on a professional show."

"But we can be professional," Sasha protested. "We did a great job yesterday."

"I'm sorry," Mr. Mazzei said. "That's my final decision."

Once they were all out in the hallway, Cloe turned to Cameron. "Can you believe he kicked us off tomorrow's show?"

Cameron shrugged. "That's fine with me," he said. "This show has been taking up too much time." He headed off toward his locker.

"How can he be happy about this?" Yasmin cried. "This is the worst thing that could've happened!"

"We're definitely not going to win the contest now." Sasha agreed.

"It might even destroy our journalism grades," Jade added. "Why would you do this to us, Tamara?"

"I keep telling you it wasn't my fault!" Tamara shouted. "I never even wanted to go on-camera to begin with!" Her eyes filled with tears, and she ran off down the hall.

Jade sighed. "I guess I was a little hard on her."

"I don't know, Jade," Sasha said. "Tamara messed up pretty bad."

"But why would she tell such a big lie?" Yasmin asked. "Why would she sabotage us like that?"

Chapter 6

"Okay, we're all here," Jade said to her friends as they all powwowed in the girls' room. "We have to figure out what happened. I know our script didn't say the money was stolen."

"The script was totally perfect," Sasha said. "Tamara just made up that stuff about the money being gone."

"But why would she do that?" Cloe asked. "It's her grade, too."

"Do you think she just doesn't like us?" Yasmin asked, sounding hurt.

"She's *never* seemed to like us," Jade pointed

out. "Ever since she joined our team, she's kept to herself. She voted against our format, she didn't come shopping with us—"

"And she was totally unhelpful during my interview with Koby," Cloe put in.

"She keeps telling us it's not her fault," Sasha interjected. "Why not give her the opportunity to explain? Does anyone know where she is?"

The girls all shook their heads. "I haven't seen her since she ran off this morning," Yasmin said.

"Me either," Jade said. "Where does she usually spend her lunch period?"

"I don't know," Cloe answered. "Maybe we should split up and look for her. I'll check the cafeteria."

"Good idea. I'll look in the art and music rooms," Sasha offered.

"I'll check out the courtyard," Jade said.

"I'll look in the library," Yasmin said. "She's so quiet, I wouldn't be surprised to find her there." She straightened her newsboy cap, then took off to find Tamara.

Yasmin tiptoed through the library and found Tamara at a table way in the back, with her nose buried in a book.

"Hey, girl," Yasmin said. She slid into a seat across from Tamara. "We need to talk."

Tamara swiped at her eyes. She looked like she'd been crying.

"Do you really want to talk? Or do you want to yell at me some more?"

"I'm just trying to understand what happened this morning," Yasmin said. "Why did you sabotage us like that?"

"I didn't," Tamara said. "I told you, I just read from the teleprompter."

"But why did you read it if you knew it was wrong?" Yasmin asked. Tamara's claims just didn't make sense.

"I wasn't paying attention to the words," Tamara admitted. "I just read them without even thinking."

"What do you mean?" Yasmin asked.

Tamara looked down at her hands. "I was terrified in front of the camera. I have horrible stage fright. That's why I voted against doing the group format."

Yasmin gasped. "You should have told us you were afraid to go on-camera!"

"We voted, and I lost," Tamara said. "It wouldn't be fair to the rest of you if I insisted on doing it my way."

"But you could've worked behind the scenes with Cam if you were that scared," Yasmin said.

"You didn't need me back there. Cameron had it covered," Tamara said. "And I knew you really wanted five girls on-screen so it would feel like a big group discussion. It was such an awesome idea, I didn't want to ruin it."

"Wow," Yasmin said. "You're really a team

player." To think—all this time the girls thought Tamara was unfriendly, when really she was just shy.

"The only way I could get through it was to just concentrate on reading the words," Tamara explained. "I was so afraid of messing up. You girls are great at going off the script and talking like you're not onstage. But all I can do is stick to what's written and try not to look stupid."

"You didn't look stupid at all!" Yasmin said. "And you contributed to our discussion about gym suits yesterday. That wasn't from the script."

Tamara blushed. "I know. I could hardly believe I did it."

"You were good at it," Yasmin told her. "I bet if you tried it more often, you'd get even better."

"I don't know," Tamara said. "I've always been kind of shy. But you and Jade were having such a fun discussion that, for a second, I forgot the camera was even on."

"See?" Yasmin said. "Maybe if you hang out with us more, you'd be more comfortable talking to us on-camera. I feel shy sometimes, too, but when I'm just chatting with my girls, I don't have to stress about saying the right thing. That's the only reason we can ad-lib with each other on the show—we just act like we're having a normal conversation off-camera."

Tamara smiled. "I guess I could try that."

"*If* Mr. Mazzei ever lets us back on-camera," Yasmin said, bummed. "I can't believe he won't let us do the show tomorrow."

"I feel really awful about that," Tamara said. "Maybe I could talk to him?"

Yasmin could tell that Tamara really hadn't said the wrong line on purpose. But that could mean only one thing: Someone had put the wrong words on the teleprompter.

"We're gonna have to figure this out, first," Yasmin said. "Until we do, it won't do any good to talk to Mr. Mazzei again. We need evidence. Do you want to help us get it?"

Tamara hesitated. "I won't get in the way?"

"No way!" Yasmin cried. "You're our teammate. And, hopefully, our new friend."

"Do you mean it?" Tamara asked, smiling. "Then I'm definitely in!"

Chapter 7

"Check out this top!" Jade exclaimed. She pulled a pink leather halter top from the rack at Funky Fashions. "It's perfect with your red hair, Tamara!"

"And it goes with the slammin' jeans we found for you at Tokyo-a-Go-Go," Sasha said.

"You really think I can wear an outfit like this?" Tamara asked, holding the top against herself as she looked in the mirror.

"Totally!" Cloe said. "You already have cool

clothes and you know how to wear them. We're just showing you how to put them together in even cooler ways."

"You girls make fashion seem so easy," Tamara said.

"It *is* easy," Yasmin answered. "Too bad it won't be so simple to fix our problem in journalism class."

"All day long people were asking me why we messed up so bad," Sasha said.

"We have to figure out what went wrong!" Jade said.

"If Tamara read the teleprompter right,

that means the words on the teleprompter were the problem," Sasha said.

"So the script was wrong," Cloe said.

"But I wrote the whole script, and I know I didn't say the money for the France trip was gone," Yasmin said.

"Somebody must have changed the script!" Sasha cried.

"But nobody touched the script except us," Cloe pointed out.

"And Cameron," Jade said. "I gave him the script right before we went on. He had to make my changes on the teleprompter."

"Well, Cameron didn't mess up our script," Cloe said. "I'm sure he only changed what he was supposed to change."

"Yeah. He's on our team, so he couldn't have done it," Tamara said.

"Plus, he's one of our best friends," Sasha added. She pulled out her PDA and clicked it on. "Let's make a list of people who might want us to do a bad job on our report."

"How about Kath?" Cloe asked. "She's so competitive about the journalism project. And she's been doing a terrible job on our makeup. Remember when she poked Tamara in the eye? It's like she wants us to look bad."

"And she thought you chose me for your team over her," Tamara reminded them. "Maybe she's mad about that."

Sasha wrote Kath's name on the suspect list.

"I hate to say this," Jade put in, "but maybe Cameron really does need to be on the list, too."

"No way!" Cloe protested.

"He is the last one who had the script before we went on the air," Yasmin said gently.

"And he's been acting totally weird the last few days," Sasha said. "He's so into getting that internship that he can't be bothered with our show. Maybe he sabotaged us so that he'd have more time to concentrate on his music class."

Cloe bit her lip. She hated to think Cameron could do such a thing to them. But her friends had a point. He *had* been acting strange. "Cameron also complained about doing all the work while we had all the on-screen fun," she said. "I guess he could be jealous that he never gets to go on-camera."

"That might have made him want to sabotage us," Jade put in.

"I know we don't want to think anything bad about one of our friends," Yasmin said. "But we have to face it: Cameron is a suspect."

Chapter 8

"Morning," Sasha grumbled on Wednesday.

"What's wrong, Bunny Boo?" Jade asked.

"I'm in charge of the teleprompter today," Sasha said. "And I just took a look at the script. A lot of it's about our report yesterday."

Cloe frowned. "Does it say we did a bad job?"

Sasha nodded. "It apologizes for the confusion we caused."

"Oh, no," Tamara commiserated from behind them. The girls turned around—and gasped. Tamara looked totally different. Blond highlights gleamed in her red hair. She wore a little bit of makeup, applied just the way they had taught her yesterday. And she looked totally chic in flared jeans and an Indian-print tunic.

"You look amazing!" Cloe cried.

Tamara grinned. "I feel amazing. I had a great time hanging with you yesterday. I wish I could have had this much fun working with you before we got kicked off the show." She sighed. "I can't stop thinking about how this disaster is all my fault! I should never have read the wrong info."

"It's not your fault," Yasmin told her. "Whoever changed the script is responsible."

"Can we get some makeup for our anchorperson?" Kath demanded, bursting in on their group. "We've been waiting."

"Oh, sorry." Yasmin rushed over to the makeup chair. It was her job today.

Kath stood around watching while Yasmin did the anchorperson's makeup. "Our team is definitely going to win the contest now," Kath bragged. "We had great ratings when it was our turn before. That's why Mr. Mazzei chose us to do the report today. We're so good, he wants you to learn from us!"

Yasmin tried to ignore her. Sure, Kath's team was good. But Kath herself never even went on-camera. So why was she the one who bragged all the time? Yasmin had an idea. Kath was on their suspect list, and all the girls were desperate to clear Cameron's name. Maybe she should start the investigation right now.

"How come you never go on-camera?" she asked Kath. "Are you camera-shy like Tamara?"

"No way!" Kath cried. "I'm just not our anchorperson."

"Who decided that you would have only one anchor?" Yasmin asked.

Kath shrugged. "It didn't occur to us to do it any other way."

"So why weren't you the one who got picked?" Yasmin prodded.

Kath lowered her eyes, looking embarrassed. "We voted, and someone else won," she whispered. Then, as if trying to convince herself, she added, "I'm cool with it, though."

"But wouldn't you like to try being the anchor, even just one time?" Yasmin insisted.

Kath blushed a little. "Yeah. I think I'd be really good at it. But when we get superhigh ratings for today's show and win the contest, my team will have a weekly slot on *Rise and Shine*. Then I'll get my chance."

"Three, two, one," the producer counted down. "We're on. Teleprompter!"

Sasha hit a button on the computer that ran the teleprompter. As words began scrolling down the big screen on top of it, she wondered how things could have gone so wrong the day before. After all, she and Yasmin had loaded the script into the teleprompter computer themselves. The only other person who had touched it was

Cameron, when he had to fix that wrong number.

Sasha looked around for Cameron. He was standing with Cloe, helping her hold the boom mike. It was a microphone on a long pole that had to be held over the anchorperson's head to pick up her voice, and it was very heavy.

Leave it to Cameron to help Cloe, Sasha thought with a smile. Cameron was such a cool guy. And he was totally crushing on Cloe. It made no sense for him to want to ruin their show. It was time for Sasha to try to get to the bottom of the issue.

When the broadcast ended, she went straight over to Cameron. "Okay, Cameron, what do you know about the teleprompter mess-up yesterday?" she demanded.

Chapter 9

"I hope you're not suggesting that I was behind yesterday's disaster," Cameron said. "Because that would be totally insulting."

"Sasha!" Cloe cried. "We don't have any real evidence."

"It's just that you seem so much more interested in getting that internship than in our show," Jade said.

"*And* you've been complaining about how much time this show takes," Yasmin added.

"How can you guys think I'd do that to you?" Cameron cried. "I'm on your team!"

"But you didn't care when we got taken off the air today," Yasmin said. "Just tell us the truth, Cameron. Did you put in the part about the France trip being canceled?"

Hearing their friends' raised voices, Tamara and Eitan rushed over. "What's going on?" Tamara asked.

"I'm wondering the same thing," said Mr. Mazzei. "Because this arguing is *not* convincing me of your ability to behave professionally." He frowned at them.

"The reason we messed up our report yesterday is because Tamara read straight from the teleprompter—and the script in the teleprompter was the wrong script!" Cloe said.

"Somebody must have changed it before we

went on the air," Jade added.

"And we're just trying to figure out who it was by asking some of the people involved," Yasmin said.

"Look, Mr. Mazzei, our entire script was stored on my PDA, just in case we needed a backup," Sasha said. She pulled it out of her bag, clicked it on, and scrolled to their original script. "See? In the original script, it doesn't say anything about the trip funds being stolen."

Mr. Mazzei turned to Cameron. "This script is correct. Obviously, somebody did change it. And Cameron, weren't you the one who had the script last?"

Everyone silently stared at Cameron, waiting for an answer. As much as the girls wanted to clear their names, they still didn't want to see their friend get in trouble.

"Well, I—" Cameron muttered, hanging his head guiltily.

"This doesn't look good, Cameron," Mr. Mazzei said. "Sabotaging your classmates' work is a terrible thing to do. If this is true, I'm going to have to fail you."

Sasha, Jade, and Yasmin all bowed their heads in silence while Cloe tried to think of something, anything, she could say in her friend's defense.

"Wait, Mr. Mazzei!" a voice cried from the back of the studio. Everyone turned around to see Kath running toward the group. "Don't fail Cameron! I'm the one who did it. I changed their script in the teleprompter."

Chapter 10

Everybody gasped.

"You did it?" Jade cried. "But how?"

"Kath was in charge of running the teleprompter yesterday," Cameron said. "And she offered to make the change for me."

"So you gave her the script?" Cloe asked.

Cameron nodded. "I should have made the change myself. It was my job. But I wanted to double-check my music theory homework before the next class." He blushed right up to his blond hair. "That internship is really important to me. But not so important that I would sabotage our team just to get out of doing the work."

"I'm sorry I accused you," Sasha said.

"We should've known you would never do something like that," Cloe said.

"So you put the false info in?" Yasmin asked Kath.

"Are you really that competitive?" Jade demanded.

"No," Kath said. "I just wanted to get on-camera. I didn't get to be the anchor on my team. But you guys put everybody onscreen! I figured if we could win the contest and get a slot on *Rise and Shine*, maybe I could convince the rest of my team to use your format. Then I'd get to be on TV, too."

"So you sabotaged us because you wanted

to get on-camera?" Yasmin asked, confused.

"Why was being on-camera so important to you?" Eitan asked.

Kath blushed. "I've never told anybody, but I've always dreamed of being a TV news anchor," she said. "I'm really sorry. I know I shouldn't have done it."

"You need to go to the principal's office and tell him what you did," Mr. Mazzei said sternly.

Cloe turned to her friends. "I guess we're not in trouble anymore," she said.

Tamara, Sasha, and Jade nodded.

"So why aren't we happier?" asked Yasmin.

Chapter 11

Right after class, the girls went straight to the principal's office. Kath was just leaving.

"What happened?" Cloe asked.

"I told the principal not to blame you, and that you deserve another chance," Kath said.

"Thanks," Jade said. "But I think what Cloe meant is . . . what happened to *you*?"

"I got two weeks of detention," Kath said.

"Bummer," Sasha said.

"I deserve it. What I did was wrong," Kath said. "No matter how much I wanted to get on-camera."

The girls smiled at one another. They were all thinking the same thing.

"It's your lucky day, girlfriend!" Jade said. "You can be the guest commentator on our show tomorrow!"

"Really?" Kath cried. "You would do that for me, after what I did to you?"

"Totally. It's obvious you'd make an awesome hard-nosed reporter," Yasmin said.

"I'll do your makeup and hair," Jade offered.

"And I'll bring in my electric-blue hoodie," Tamara added. "It will make your eyes really pop on-camera."

Yasmin gave Sasha a wink. Tamara had really come out of her shell!

"It'll be our best show yet!" Cloe said.

" ... And that's the style news from Stiles High," Tamara said on Friday morning. She smiled confidently into the camera. "We had a fabulous week. Hope you did, too!"

"And ... we're off the air," Cameron announced.

"That was a great show!" Jade cried.

"You did a great job, Tamara!" Yasmin said.

Tamara blushed. "Being on-camera still makes me nervous, but you guys are so good at it that I just try to follow your lead."

"She's right," Mr. Mazzei said, coming up to the girls. "You're talk-show naturals. Your team has won the contest. You get the weekly spot on *Rise and Shine!*"

"I know what our first story is going to be—a report on everything we did on our amazing class trip to France!" Yasmin cried. "We'll give the hippest travel advice ever!"

"Absolutely!" Jade exclaimed. "We can report on all the new fashions."

"And the hottest music," Sasha added.

"And the most gorgeous works of art," Cloe chimed in.

"And the awesome company!" Tamara finished, her face lighting up with a smile.

The girls linked arms as they strolled out of the studio and headed off with their fellow news anchor—and new friend!